Twice-Upon-a-Time

Twice

EP PRESS
BRATTLEBORO VT

Upon-a-Time
Born and Adopted

Text by
Eleanora Patterson

Illustrations by
Barbara Ernst Prey

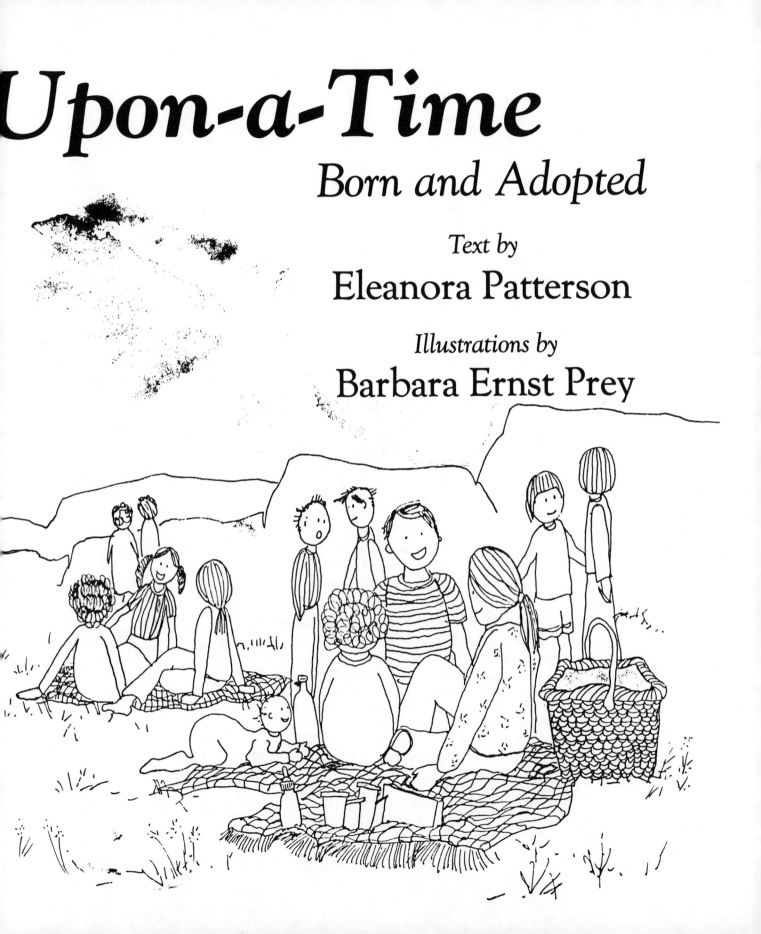

ISBN 0-9607432-1-9
Library of Congress Catalog Number 87-92071

Copyright © by Eleanora Patterson
and Barbara Ernst Prey, 1987

Designed by James F. Brisson
Williamsville, Vermont

EP PRESS
Brattleboro, Vermont 05301
Manufactured in the USA

Library of Congress Cataloging-in-Publication Data

Patterson, Eleanora, 1941–
    Twice-upon-a-time.

    Summary: Describes, in simple text and illustrations, both the
biological and social beginnings of adopted children.

    1. Adoption—Juvenile literature.   2. Children, Adopted—
Family relationships—Juvenile literature.   3. Human reproduction—
Juvenile literature.
[1. Adoption. 2. Reproduction]   I. Prey, Barbara Ernst, ill.
II. Title
HV875.P37   1987   362.7′34   87-92071
ISBN 0-9607432-1-9 (pbk.)

Do you know how wonderful you are?
You are wonderful
in being you,
the only one
who is just that you.

You are wonderful, too
in that you
are very much like
everyone else.

The story of you
has much that is true
for only you
and much that is true for others, too.

And the story of you
tells how you grew
into the wonderful you
you are now.

Everyone is given birth
by two parents,
and so were you.

And some have other parents, too.
Parents, who are family for a time,
parents, who are family for life.

You are one of many,
who have other parents;
one of many,
who were adopted
into a family for life.

Your story begins with a tiny spot
much smaller than this dot

.

This tiny beginning
was the meeting
of one of your birth mother's eggs
with one of your birth father's sperm
deep inside her body.

The egg-sperm nestled in her womb.
and grew . . .

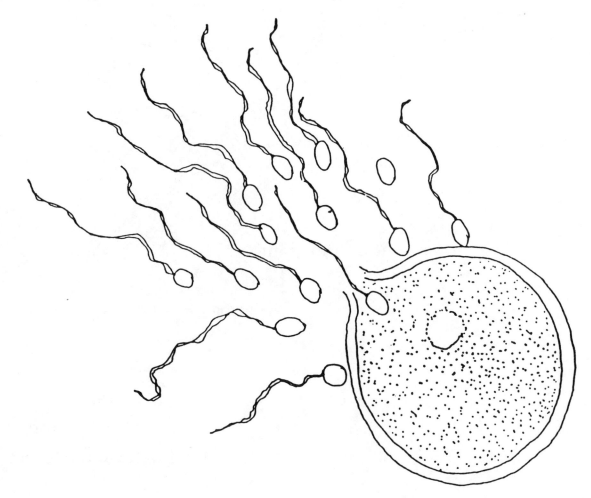

and grew.

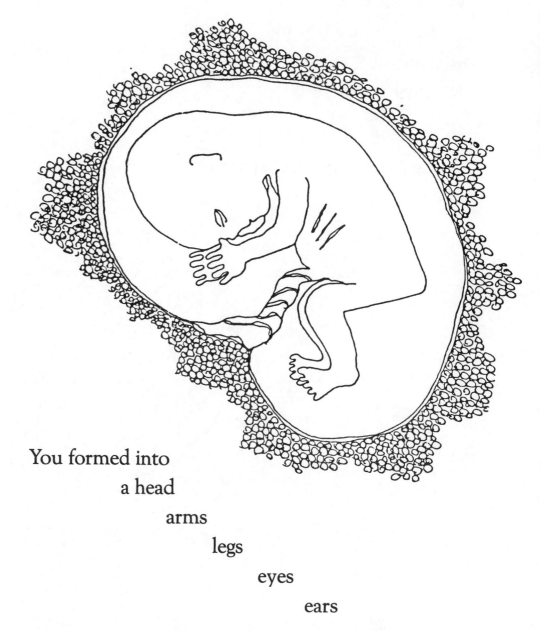

You formed into
a head
arms
legs
eyes
ears
nose
ten fingers and ten toes.

You grew,
and so did your birth mother,
as her womb stretched
to make room for you.

As you grew and grew,
there was less and less space
for you
in her womb.

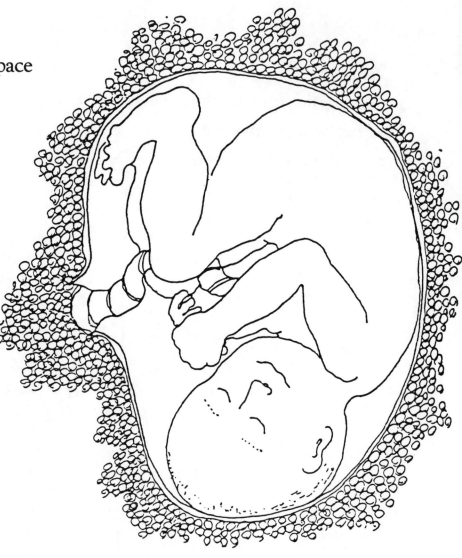

Soon, you would have to leave.

The womb is a strong muscle,
that pushed you
            and pushed you

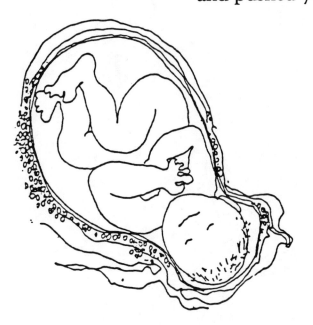

as it opened into
        the birth passage.

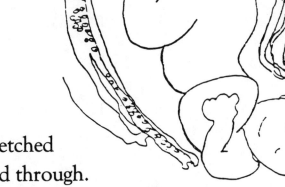

The birth passage stretched
and let you be pushed through.

Out came you!
You were born!

Your birth mother
worked hard
in giving birth to you.

And you worked hard, too,
in being born.

When you arrived,
You were very small
and very new.

You needed
Someone to hold you and feed you,
someone to wash you and comfort you
and put you to bed.

Night and day
day and night

you needed someone to care for you.

All children do.

But there came a time
when your birth mother
        your birth father
could not take care of their child
in the many, many ways parents must.

Neither one could be there
day and night
night and day
to hold and feed their child
to comfort, teach and play.

There are many reasons
why birth parents
cannot be parents
to their child for life.

Some are too young
            too sick
            too lonely

Some have too many children already.

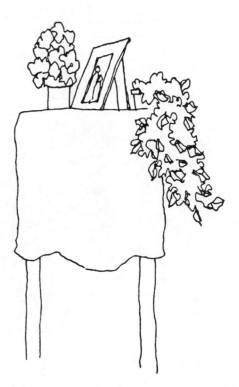

Whatever reasons birth parents have
are a truth about them
and only them
and have nothing to do
with their child.

What happened to you
has happened to many others, too.

Some children
are not even born
Some are a week or a year
or even more
when it becomes clear
when birth parents decide
they cannot be parents to their child.

Night and day
day and night,
you needed someone
to take care of you
as all children do.

And a family was found,
a family found you.

Some families, called foster families,
can give a child
a safe and caring place for a time.
Some families
can give a child
a safe and caring place for life.

You became part of a family
who had wanted very much
and worked very hard
to make their wish
for a child
come true,
and that child was you.

Their wish began tiny yet strong
to share their home
with a child
or one child more
whom they could care for.

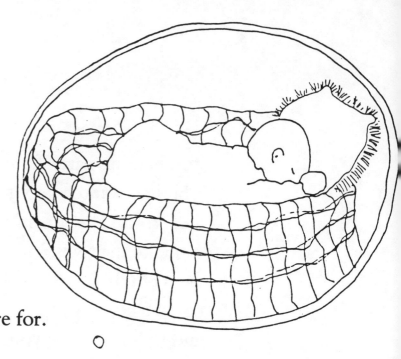

Their wish grew and grew
as they became sure
they had enough love
and all it takes
to care for a child
no matter what.

As they waited,
they made plans
and talked to others,
who could help them.

Until,
the day came

the day you were welcomed
the day you welcomed
your family for life.

Your adoption was a special day
for each and every one of you.

Some children are adopted
when they are born
some are one, two or four,
some children are eight years old
and more.

Much that is true
about your family and you
is true
of other families, too.

Your mother,
your father,
one or both
take care of you.
They help to feed you,
they care what happens
and they share special things
they like to do
         with you.

And you help, too.

You share
your smiles and tears
and hurts.
As you learn
and play and work,
you help
because you are you.

Each and every day
you know a little more
you grow a little more.

And somedays,
you do something
you never did before.

Once you could only crawl, then walk,
then climb upstairs and down.

Your sounds became words:
one
　　two
　　　　a few
　　　　　　then many.

Now you can run and jump.
You can tell of what you see
and imagine whatever you might be.

And you can ask questions
and try to find out
about everything
and anything
you want.

Sometimes
children who are adopted
wonder about their birth parents

Maybe you do, too.

Some children wonder
what their birth parents are like
　　　　　　　　how they look
　　　　　　　　what they do
or what it would be like to live
　　　　　　　　with their birth mother
　　　　　　　　their birth father, too.

Some children want to find out
all they can
about their birth parents.
And some children do not
now
or ever.

It is fine
if you want to find out
more about your birth parents
and the story of you.

And it is fine, too,
if you do not.

Day and night
night and day
you keep growing and growing
in being you
and part of your family.

And the story of you
keeps growing, too,
as it tells what happens
            and what you do
            and know
            and feel

in being the wonderful you
you are.

Eleanora Patterson is an author, student of communications, and financial planner. Her previous writings include *Becoming*, a poetic book for young children about their biological beginnings, and an essay in the anthology, *Reweaving the Web of Life*. She lives in Brattleboro, VT with her husband and daughter.

Barbara Ernst Prey is an illustrator and recipient of both a Fullbright and a Luce scholarship. Her illustrations appear regularly in magazines, such as *The New Yorker*, *Gourmet Magazine*, and *The National Review*. Recently, she became an aunt to an adopted, bi-racial baby girl.